HICKORY, DICKORY, DOCK

ROBIN MULLER ; SUZANNE DURANCEAU

HICKORY, DICKORY, DOCK

Scholastic Canada Ltd.

Scholastic Canada Ltd.
123 Newkirk Road, Richmond Hill, Ontario, Canada L4C 3G5

Scholastic Inc.
555 Broadway, New York, NY 10012, USA

Ashton Scholastic Pty. Limited
PO Box 579, Gosford, NSW 2250, Australia

Ashton Scholastic Limited
Private Bag 92801, Penrose, Auckland, New Zealand

Scholastic Publications Ltd.
Villiers House, Clarendon Avenue, Leamington Spa,
Warwickshire CV32 5PR, UK

8 7 6 5 4 3 2 1   Printed in Canada   5 6 7 8/9

Canadian Cataloguing in Publication Data

Muller, Robin
Hickory, dickory, dock

ISBN 0-590-73089-4

I. Duranceau, Suzanne. II. Title.

PS8576.U44H5 1994   jC813'.54   C95-930251-4
PZ10.3.M8Hi 1994

To Lauren and Adam Traversy.
And to their brother Michael, who came just in time.
RM

To Alma and Sébastien.
And to my friends and assistants,
Tom Kapas and Luc Melanson,
with special thanks for their valuable contributions.
SD

Hickory, dickory, dock,
The cat has hidden the clock.
The clock struck one,
The hunt's begun.
Hickory, dickory, dock.

Gigglety, figglety, fare,
The goat looked under the chair.
The clock struck two,
The mouse yelled, "Boo!"
Gigglety, figglety, fare.

Margery, bargery, bow,
The monkey stubbed his toe.
The clock struck three,
He spilled the tea.
Margery, bargery, bow.

Tottery, pottery, pum,
The goat fell over the drum.
The clock struck four,
The mouse laughed, "More!"
Tottery, pottery, pum.

Hunkery, dunkery, day,
The lamb slid in on the tray.
The clock struck five,
The wolf arrived.
Hunkery, dunkery, day.

Tumberly, bumberly, boo,
The wolf fell into the glue.
The clock struck six,
He cried, "It sticks!"
Tumberly, bumberly, boo.

Ziggity, tiggity, tore,
The cow went through the floor.
The clock struck seven,
She fell from heaven.
Ziggity, tiggity, tore.

Higglety, pigglety, pot,
The goat untangled the knot.
The clock struck eight,
The cat cried, "Wait!"
Higglety, pigglety, pot.

Cattery, battery, bash,
The clock came down with a crash.
The clock struck nine,
"The fault is mine."
Cattery, battery, bash.

Rackety, knackety, knob,
They all began to sob.
The clock clunked ten,
"I'll fix it again!"
Rackety, knackety, knob.

Fiddlety, biddlety, bime,
The mouse repaired the time.
The clock struck eleven,
And all was forgiven.
Fiddlety, biddlety, bime.

Hickory, dickory, date,
"It's time to celebrate!"
The midnight hour
Has magic power . . .

Hickory, dickory, date.